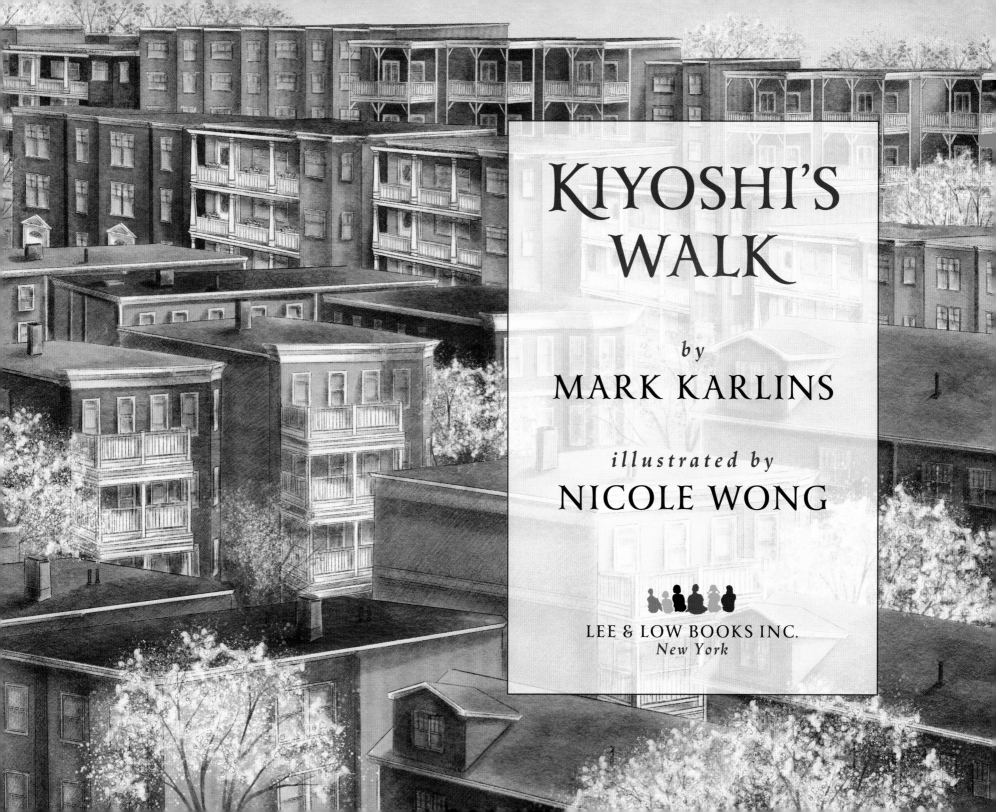

KIYOSHI'S WALK

by

MARK KARLINS

illustrated by

NICOLE WONG

LEE & LOW BOOKS INC.
New York

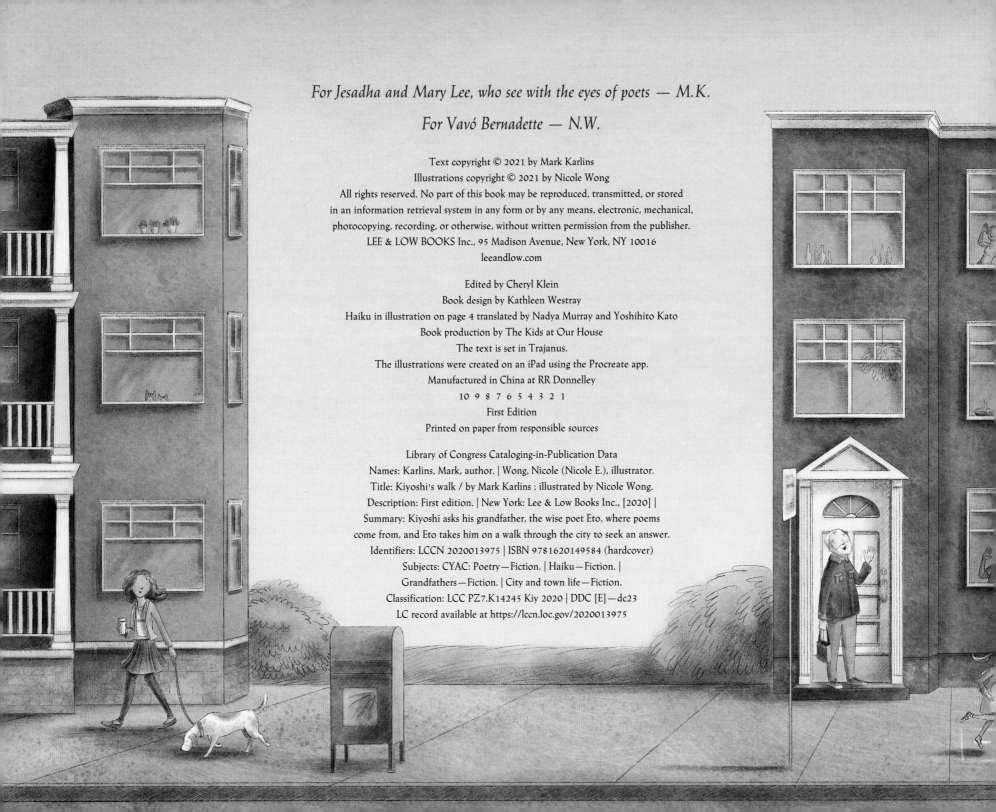

For Jesadha and Mary Lee, who see with the eyes of poets — M.K.

For Vavó Bernadette — N.W.

Edited by Cheryl Klein
Book design by Kathleen Westray
Haiku in illustration on page 4 translated by Nadya Murray and Yoshihito Kato
Book production by The Kids at Our House
The text is set in Trajanus.
The illustrations were created on an iPad using the Procreate app.
Manufactured in China at RR Donnelley
10 9 8 7 6 5 4 3 2 1
First Edition
Printed on paper from responsible sources

Library of Congress Cataloging-in-Publication Data
Names: Karlins, Mark, author. | Wong, Nicole (Nicole E.), illustrator.
Title: Kiyoshi's walk / by Mark Karlins ; illustrated by Nicole Wong.
Description: First edition. | New York: Lee & Low Books Inc., [2020] |
Summary: Kiyoshi asks his grandfather, the wise poet Eto, where poems
come from, and Eto takes him on a walk through the city to seek an answer.
Identifiers: LCCN 2020013975 | ISBN 9781620149584 (hardcover)
Subjects: CYAC: Poetry—Fiction. | Haiku—Fiction. |
Grandfathers—Fiction. | City and town life—Fiction.
Classification: LCC PZ7.K14245 Kiy 2020 | DDC [E]—dc23
LC record available at https://lccn.loc.gov/2020013975

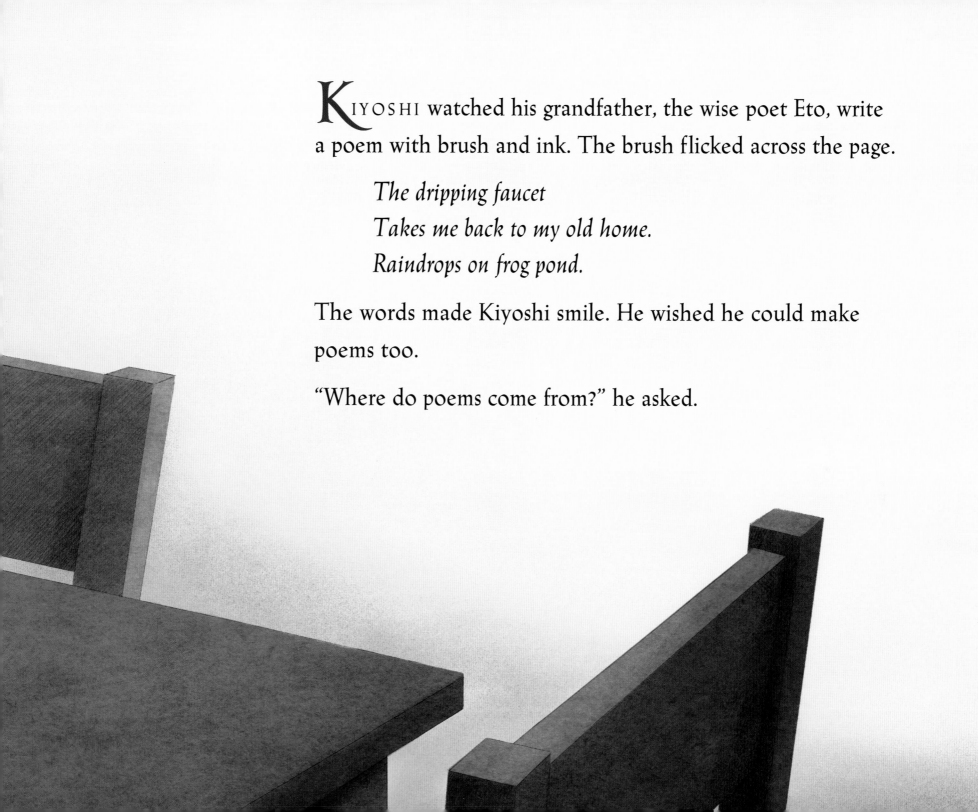

KIYOSHI watched his grandfather, the wise poet Eto, write a poem with brush and ink. The brush flicked across the page.

The dripping faucet
Takes me back to my old home.
Raindrops on frog pond.

The words made Kiyoshi smile. He wished he could make poems too.

"Where do poems come from?" he asked.

Eto put his brush and ink away.

"Let's go for a walk," he said.

He tucked a pen and paper in his pocket
and took Kiyoshi's hand.

They walked by the store on the corner.

The sun shone out from behind a cloud.

Eto stopped and wrote:

> *Hill of orange suns.*
> *Cat leaps. Oranges tumble.*
> *The cat licks his paw.*

Kiyoshi felt puzzled. "Does that mean poems come from seeing things?"

They kept walking. Kiyoshi noticed
a flower growing out of a crack in
the sidewalk. A girl whooshed by
on roller skates. At a sound,
Kiyoshi and Eto looked up.

Eto wrote:

The sky calls to us —
Pigeons, the whir of feathers.
Our arms could be wings.

"Oh," said Kiyoshi, "you find poems by listening."

They passed by an old house
with a tall wall around it.

They peeked through a crack, but
could see only a stuffed bear on the ground.

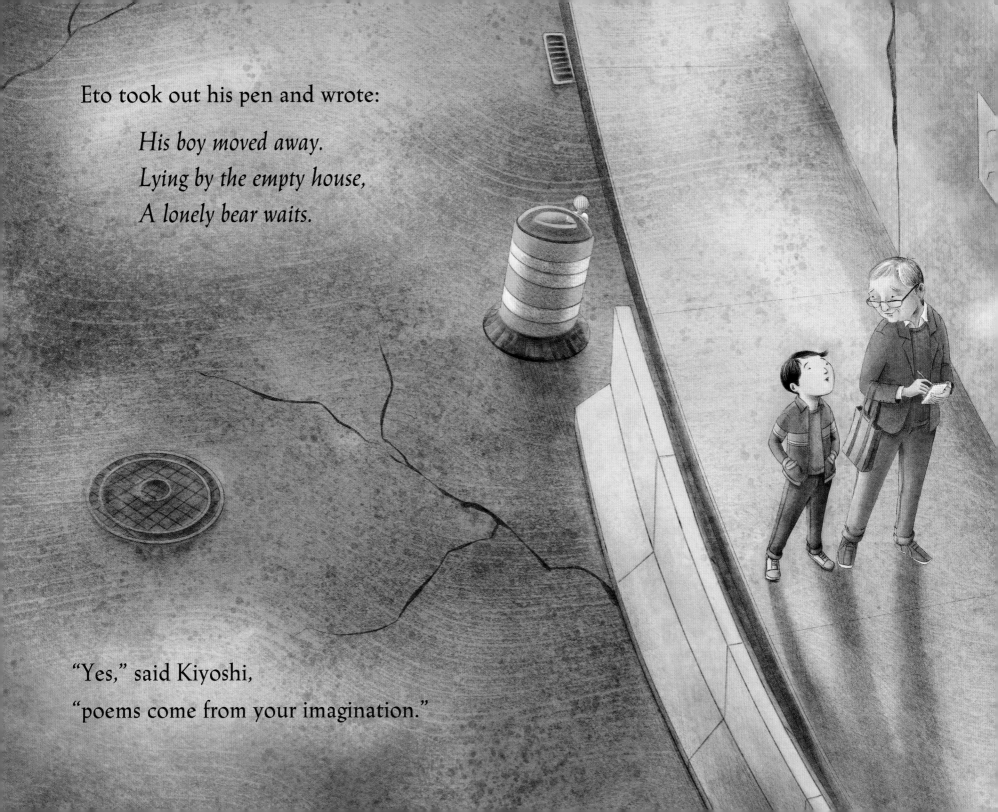

Eto took out his pen and wrote:

His boy moved away.
Lying by the empty house,
A lonely bear waits.

"Yes," said Kiyoshi,

"poems come from your imagination."

Finally, Kiyoshi and Eto reached the river. Eto sat under a tree while Kiyoshi fed crackers to some ducks. He felt a damp breeze as the sun drifted lower.

Two children reeled in their kites and left the park. Kiyoshi felt a little lonely. He told his grandfather.

Eto wrote one more poem, his hand
a shadow in the fading light:

> *Dark sky, clouded moon.*
> *Back at home, his mother's voice.*
> *A tired boy dreams.*

"I know something else," Kiyoshi said.

"Our feelings also make poems."

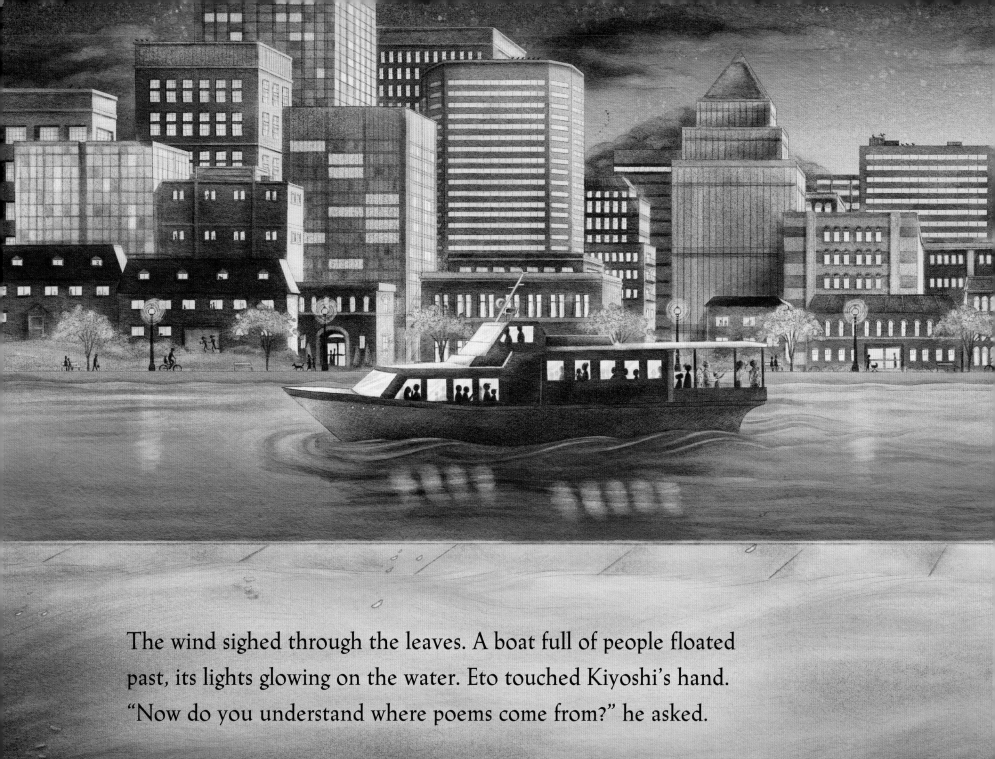

The wind sighed through the leaves. A boat full of people floated past, its lights glowing on the water. Eto touched Kiyoshi's hand. "Now do you understand where poems come from?" he asked.

Kiyoshi thought for a few seconds. "They come from here," he said, and opened his arms wide to take in the river and the sky and the distant buildings. "And they come from here," he said, and pointed to his own heart.

"Yes," said Eto, "and they come from the way the two come together." He brought his hands close, touching one to the other.

They sat for a moment in silence.

"May I write a poem?" Kiyoshi asked.

Eto nodded.

Kiyoshi took a deep breath and wrote:

> *In the cool spring night*
> *The wind's dance makes me shiver.*
> *Your voice keeps me warm.*

Eto read his grandson's poem. He smiled.

Kiyoshi slipped his hand into his grandfather's. Under
the streetlights, they began their long walk home. And in
everything there was a poem: the faces of the people, the
sound of the river, the moon breaking from the clouds.

Author's Note

MY OWN LIFE AS A WRITER began with poetry. I wondered, like Kiyoshi, how to find poems of my own and how to write them.

Kiyoshi and Eto are both fictional characters. But their poems, called haiku, are a traditional form that originated in Japan. The most famous writer of haiku was Basho, a Japanese poet who lived from 1644 to 1694. I like to think that Eto is similar to Basho in that both are keen observers of the world.

Haiku do not use rhyme, and they often concentrate on ordinary, "unpoetic" things: taking a walk, brushing your teeth, toast popping from the toaster, a crumpled newspaper blowing down the street. The focus is on the moment. Often the final line of a haiku has an unexpected image, a surprise.

A haiku is always written in three lines. Haiku in English commonly have five syllables in the first line, seven in the second, and five in the third (a total of seventeen syllables). In the original Japanese, it's not syllables that matter, but sounds. In English, some poets reflect this by choosing a looser style, writing three-line poems that do not conform to the five-seven-five pattern, but capture the spirit of the haiku by focusing on nature, spontaneity, and simplicity of expression.

Usually created by a single poet, haiku can become part of a gamelike form called renga in which two or more people write linked poems. Haiku can also include painting and calligraphy. If we look with a poet's eye, everything becomes poetry.